Alex and Cookie and the Creeper Army

(an unofficial Minecraft adventure)

Book 2 of the *Adventures of Alex and Cookie*

By,
Blockerella

Table of Contents

Chapter 1..1

Chapter 2..7

Chapter 3...13

Chapter 4...19

Chapter 5...22

Chapter 6...29

Chapter 7...34

Chapter 8...42

Chapter 9...47

Chapter 10..54

Chapter 11..61

Chapter 12..68

Chapter 13..74

About Blockerella......................................80

Chapter 1

Alex and Cookie were in the garden harvesting some carrots one fine spring morning. Cookie was very helpful with this task. She put her paws around the base of the carrot, grabbed the top with her teeth and then with one smooth jerk, pulled up the carrot. She could go down a whole row in minutes.

Cookie's kittens played just beyond the garden on a wide patch of green grass. Alex had mined a few blocks of dirt and grass and lined them up in a square shape. This made a kind of up and down obstacle course for the kittens to run on. They raced around and around, each trying to be the leader.

Alex had named the one girl and two boys, Sugar, Chip and Bob.

Occasionally, Alex had to stop her work and watch them romp. They were so cute! Sugar was yellow and orange like her mother, Chip was chocolate colored spots and Bob was a tuxedo of grey and white.

Out of the bunch, Bob was definitely the most mischievous. He would trick his brother and sister into going one direction and then circle around and grab their tales.

Often at dinner time he often would send them looking in all directions for a lost toy and then steal their food. When Sugar and Chip would return from the wild goose chase, Bob would sit looking content, licking his little white mitten paws.

Alex couldn't help herself and laughed as she saw Cookie try and round up the playful kittens and put them in the house. Bob was rolling back and forth on the grass with an egg in his paws. Cookie finally walked over and whacked it away.

The egg landed with a thud on the grass, broke open and a new white chicken came out. Alex had recently added a chicken coop to her property and had five fine white hens. She quickly went over to the chicken and herded it into the enclosure.

Alex and Cookie had been home for a couple of weeks since their adventure saving Steve. After the surprise of Cookie's kittens, Alex had decided to stay on the farm for a while.

The kittens had grown quickly and were able to mostly care for themselves now. Alex had made sure to gather a large supply of fish so they would always be well fed.

She wondered if, at last, she and Cookie could go out and explore again. She had vowed that she would find new adventures out in the world. And, Cookie seemed like she could use a break!

Chapter 2

The next day, Alex made arrangements with Mr. Long Nose to check on the kittens for the few days they would be gone. Mr. Long Nose seemed eager to help even after the kittens climbed up his brown robe. They settled on his shoulders and in his folded arms. As he bobbed up and down they drifted off to sleep.

Alex decided to bring an iron pickaxe, some steaks and one of the potions she had been working on lately. She had begun experimenting with crafting potions because she thought that she might need some of these special mixes on some future adventures.

She mixed a golden carrot, a fermented spider eye and an awkward potion to make a potion of invisibility. Who knows? Maybe it would come in handy.

On the next morning, Alex and Cookie set out towards the mountains. Not sure what to do or where exactly to find "adventure," Alex had decided to visit Steve.

When she had seen him last (when she saved him!), he had told her his plans. Steve said that he was going to find the tallest peak he could, climb to the top and mine straight down.

Steve was sure that this would lead to a huge trove of emeralds. It seemed an odd thing to Alex since plenty of miners had luck going straight into a mountain at the base but she didn't argue the point.

Alex and Cookie spent the whole day on their journey. They went from their forest biome home, through the jungle, and into the desert before reaching the mountains. There were many beautiful and curious things to see in all of these areas. Alex had once seen huge mushroom shaped trees and the peculiar Mooshroom Cow.

It got colder and colder the closer they got to the mountains. Soon they were on mountain steppes that were thickly forested with bushy green trees.

They began to climb. They came to even larger and steeper areas. Soon huge blocks of exposed coal were all around them.

Alex realized they had at last arrived at the extreme hills biome.

Now where was the tallest peak? She saw one particularly tall mountain that's top was obscured by clouds. *If I can't see the top, that must be it!*, thought Alex.

Chapter 3

Alex and Cookie had stopped to rest on a block and have some steak before they continued with their journey.

As they were sitting, a bat suddenly flew over their heads. It almost crashed into them and veered away at the last second, continuing down the mountain.

As it flew, Alex could hear it saying in a scared voice, "Must hurry! Must hurry! So many...why!?"

Alex called after the bat but it didn't turn around.

Alex and Cookie started to climb again. Soon they saw more and more creatures going the opposite direction. A rabbit and a sheep all ran past them down the mountain looking terrified.

"What could be happening?" Alex asked Cookie.

Cookie replied with a *Meow* and bounded up the rocks. She was never one to run away from danger. Alex knew how brave she was and resolved to try and be just as fearless.

Soon they were near the cloud-covered peak. The base of the massive mountain was below them.

Alex looked down and saw what she thought must be

hundreds of Creepers moving out of a cave opening in the mountain! She watched in horror as they slithered out of the black hole in the mountain.

The Creepers had blank faces with permanent frowns. Their strange four-legged sliding walk sent chills down Alex's spine.

No wonder the animals were running away!, thought Alex.

Cookie let out a little *Meow* and sat down. Even she was mystified by what she saw.

Why were so many Creepers coming out of this cave? It was so strange.

The Creepers all appeared to be going in the same direction. They were following a path through the mountain and towards the mountain steppes.

Alex realized that if they continued in this direction they would go through the jungle and into the forest. They could overrun the villages and would at some point reach her home.

The kittens! Mr. Long Nose might have to flee and then who would look out for Sugar, Chip and Bob? Alex looked at Cookie. She thought Cookie must have read her mind because she looked down with a sad, *Meow*.

Chapter 4

The Creepers would most likely leave the kittens alone since they avoided Ocelots but the baby cats still needed someone to care for them.

Alex and Cookie had no choice. They had to get into that cave and find out who or what was sending the Creeper army. They could simply walk up to the cave and go in because with Cookie the Creepers would not harm them. *But*, Alex thought, *I don't want to be discovered so that I can find out who or what is sending the Creepers out of the cave.*

She had an idea. She would need to lure a Creeper to them. Alex picked up a nearby block of coal and hurled it down the hill towards the Creepers. As it bounced she quickly ducked down. The block rolled to a stop directly in a Creeper's path. Alex saw it look up in their direction.

She crossed her fingers! The Creeper turned, curious, and started its creepy glide up the hill towards them. Alex got her

diamond sword ready.

Chapter 5

The Creeper continued up the hill with its menacing eyes trained on the rock that Alex and Cookie were hiding behind. In a moment, the Creeper slid next to them.

Alex stood, swung the sword and, in one swift movement, lopped off the Creepers head! The body toppled over and the head landed on the ground. The Creeper didn't even have time to be surprised.

"Alright, Cookie," said Alex, "Let's see if this works."

Alex picked up the Creeper head and looked inside. It was hollow. It figures, she thought to herself. She slipped it on.

"What do you think?" she asked Cookie.

Cookie looked at her wide-eyed. Alex hoped that the head would be enough for them to slip past the Creepers and get into the cave. She knew Creepers were not particularly smart. Also, they rarely look down, preferring to keep their heads staring ahead.

With Alex's green tunic and brown pants, she might just be able to blend in. Cookie would have to trail behind her and try to stay out of sight.

The Creepers would not harm Cookie but it might draw more attention than they would like if they saw her.

Alex and Cookie started to make their way down to the cave.

They went from rock to rock, ducking and dodging. Some Creepers turned their heads in Alex and Cookie's direction but then continued their march after they saw Alex's Creeper head. Cookie stayed well hidden behind Alex.

At last, they were almost at the cave opening. Creepers streamed from the black hole in the mountain.

This last part, they would have to run!

Alex and Cookie dashed into the cave. It was dark and cold. Alex felt herself bump into something. She knew she was surrounded by Creepers.

She felt very afraid. Then she felt the fur of Cookie's body brush against her leg. *Phew*, Cookie was by her side.

She could see a strange bluish purple light up ahead. As they got closer, Alex saw the unmistakable tan markings and black top of an end portal!

She watched in horror as a Creeper head emerged followed by the body. When it was all the way out it stepped off of the stone. Then the next head appeared.

This was a lot worse than she could have imagined. She wondered how she could destroy the end portal and stop the Creeper apocalypse.

Alex saw yet another Creeper emerge. Then as quick as a flash she felt Cookie run by her. He jumped into the black hole and disappeared.

"Cookie, Noooo!" cried Alex as she ran after her. She paused at the edge of the black abyss for a moment, took a breath and jumped in.

Chapter 6

Alex felt a momentary blast of cold air against her skin and a sense of being weightless. It was like floating in the dark. Then she felt as though she was moving up through the darkness and into dim light.

She found herself standing on end stone next to a portal. It was strange because she didn't remember actually coming out of anything.

Alex looked around. She was surrounded by hilly terrain with large obsidian columns dotting an eerie green landscape.

Where was Cookie, Alex wondered?

Just then she heard a *Meow*. Cookie was next to an obsidian pillar in front of Alex. Alex rushed to her and patted her head.

"There you are!" she scolded then crossly asked, "What were you thinking?"

As her eyes adjusted to the light she could see movement all around her. Tall skinny black creatures with glowing purple eyes were moving in all directions.

Alex had heard about these creatures. She kept her head down and avoided their purple gaze. Slowly, Alex and Cookie made their way forward, going from column to column.

Ahead, she could see some Creepers moving away from a high platform. As they got closer, Alex realized, that there was a large Creeper-like creature wearing a tuxedo that appeared to be spawning the Creepers!

In its hands the suited creature held glowing green eggs that it smashed on the ground. The Creepers emerged fully-formed from the eggs and moved down the platform in an assembly line.

What was this thing? The only answer Alex could imagine is that it was a Griefer bent on destruction. The Griefer had taken the skin of a Creeper and dressed it up in fancy clothes.

What should she do? She couldn't think of a thing! Cookie looked up at her with her deep, black eyes.

Chapter 7

Alex took a deep breath and stepped out from behind the column.

"Hey! What are you doing?" she said in as commanding a voice as she could.

The Griefer looked up, startled. It stopped its spawning work and examined Alex.

Out of its unreadable face came a tiny, high-pitched voice that said, "How did you find me?"

"It wasn't hard with all of those Creepers coming out of the cave in the mountain," replied Alex.

"Oh yes, I guess not. Well, get out of here," it said a little peevishly, " I have work to do."

"Your work is disrupting the whole overworld!" Alex said angrily.

"That *is* my plan," said the Griefer.

Alex was getting annoyed now, "Well, you need to stop this nonsense! We live there and we have a lot to take care of."

"I don't care," said the Griefer, sounding like a spoiled child, "I'm not having any fun."

"Why aren't you having any fun?" asked Alex.

"*Because,* no one will be my friend. I can't get any animals to like me," the Griefer whined.

"Did you try and be their friend first?" asked Alex, exasperated.

"Well no, but they should just like me."

"Why?" asked Alex.

"Just because I'm great and I'm very powerful and I'll hurt them if they don't!" The Griefer was starting to sound angry now.

Just then, Cookie came out from behind the column where she had been sitting.

"An Ocelot?!" said the Griefer. "I've always wanted one of those!"

The Griefer started to lunge toward Cookie. Cookie ran one direction and then another, trying to get away.

Alex screamed, "Be careful!"

The Griefer was now near the steep sides of the End. In its manic haste to catch Cookie it didn't see how perilously close it was to the edge.

Suddenly, Alex realized that this had been Cookie's plan all along. She was leading it to the edge.

Alex saw her chance. She mined a block and just as the Griefer ran towards Cookie, and threw it in its path. The Griefer stumbled on the block, teetered forwards and then fell over the edge.

Cookie and Alex ran to where the Griefer had tripped and looked over. They could just see the green head with the frown disappearing out of sight.

As the Griefer fell, Alex heard, "Why can't we be friendssssss?"

Chapter 8

Alex patted Cookie's head as they looked down into the abyss.

As she turned around she found herself face to face with an Enderman! She tried to look away quickly but it was too late.

The Enderman's jaw dropped open and his strange garbled cry came out.

Alex and Cookies stumbled backwards in fear. Then they turned and ran towards the End

Portal. The Enderman flashed in front of them blocking their way.

Alex tried to quickly think. *What could they do?*

She suddenly remembered the invisibility potion she had put in her inventory!

Alex ran to a obsidian pillar and crouched behind it. *But where was Cookie?!* She could see her running towards the End Portal. The Enderman was close behind.

Alex screamed, "Cookie!"

The Enderman turned in Alex's direction and just as he teleported in front of her she quickly drank the potion. In an instant she was invisible.

In that very same moment, the Enderman appeared in front of her. Alex ran out of its grasp and it clutched the air, confused.

She ran to the End Portal and making sure that Cookie was next to her, she jumped in.

They had the same floating sensation as before and then emerged out of the other side of the End Portal.

Alex found her iron pickaxe and smashed the Portal as quickly as she could. Remembering the Enderman's cold eyes and the feeling of its icy black hands of death almost touching her made her shiver.

She destroyed the Portal so thoroughly that nothing was left but a hole in the ground of the cave.

Well, nothing is getting through that!, she thought.

Chapter 9

Alex and Cookie stood in the dark cave. Alex searched through her inventory and found a torch. She lit it and looked around.

Phew, at least we are alone, she thought. She followed the hollow stone corridor to the cave opening.

It was night now and she could hear the unmistakable sound of zombies nearby. Alex decided that they would have to wait until morning to figure out what to do next.

She quickly built a wall of cobblestone to cover the opening of the cave. Then she and Cookie settled down to wait out the night. Alex could tell that Cookie was worried about the kittens by the way she paced around the cave.

"Try not to worry Cookie," she told her. "They will be alright for tonight and tomorrow we will figure out what to do." Still, Alex couldn't help but be worried too.

The next morning, just as the sun was beginning to rise, Alex broke through the wall. She and Cookie began to scale the mountains they had journeyed through the day before.

They did not see any Creepers at first but Alex knew they were bound to begin to run into them.

Sure enough, as they crested a mountain and looked down into the next valley to cross, Alex could see the unmistakable dots of green moving along the terrain.

She turned to Cookie, "Go
through or go around?" she
asked.

Alex didn't have her Creeper disguise this time. Though if Cookie stayed near to she should have some protection. It was risky though. If they got separated Alex could be in trouble.

Alex got her diamond sword ready. She and Cookie boldly walked down the mountain. As they marched their way through the increasing numbers of Creepers, Alex became more and more uneasy.

The Creepers swiveled their ghoulish heads with their black eyes and frown to watch them as they went. Occasionally, one would lunge toward Alex and Cookie would run in between them.

She would let out a loud, "Meow!" and the Creeper would back away.

There were so many that Alex was now very worried. They had to get to the head of this army before it reached the forest.

She and Cookie began to run.

What would she do when she found the lead Creepers? Alex wasn't sure.

On and on, Alex and Cookie ran. At last, at the edge of the

desert, they saw the Creepers at the front of the column slithering their way into the jungle.

Chapter 10

Alex knew they had to get ahead of the Creeper army!

"Come on!" she told Cookie urgently.

They plunged into the thick trees and vines. As they were running, Alex heard a strange sound from Cookie. It was a *Meow* but she seemed to be projecting her voice through the trees. The sound echoed strangely through the air and seemed to bounce off of every leaf so that it was everywhere.

They continued through the jungle until they were on the edge of the plains which was just before the village. Cookie had *meowed* the whole way.

As they emerged from the forest, to Alex's complete astonishment, in front of them was a long line of Ocelots. It was an amazing sight. Yellow Ocelots with orange spots, jet black Ocelots, and ginger with white stripes all milled around in as much of a line as cats will make.

Cookie! She must have been calling the Ocelots of the jungle to help defend their home. Alex didn't have much time to wonder at her little cat's accomplishment.

The first Creeper emerged from the jungle. It's slither stopped in its tracks as it saw the line of cats. Its head swiveled from side to side taking in the line of Ocelots.

Slowly more and more Creepers came out of the jungle. They too, stopped at the sight of the Ocelots.

Then to Alex's amazement, the Ocelots sat up, and began to walk towards the Creepers. The Creepers turned away and began to go back into the jungle.

This continued on and on. Alex followed behind the line of Ocelots. Occasionally, a Creeper would slip around the side where the line ended. Alex used her diamond sword to quickly hack it to pieces. Alex was astounded at the bravery of these cats!

It took all day but at last the Creepers were pushed back to the extreme mountains. Up and down they went. Finally, they were at their place of origin, the cave. Alex knew the cave was very large inside and went deep into the mountain.

"Let's push them into the cave!" she told the Ocelots. They Ocelots made a circle around the Creeper horde and slowly began to advance. The only place for the Creepers to go was into the dark cave.

Soon they willingly slithered into the darkness. They couldn't get away from the Ocelots fast enough.

Finally, all but a few Creepers were in the cave.

Now to finish this, thought Alex. She pulled out some TNT from her inventory and placed it at the mouth of the cave. She lit the fuse and ran back, yelling at the Ocelots to clear the area.

A moment later there was a huge, "Boom". The mountains shook with the explosion.

Alex looked at the cave opening. It was gone. The mountain had been sealed shut with the Creeper army inside. *Hopefully they would be frozen there for all eternity,* she thought.

Chapter 11

Alex turned toward her army of Ocelots. They sat all around her and looked up at her with their deep eyes. She couldn't have been more proud and grateful to these amazing creatures. Then they all began to *Meow* happily.

Alex announced joyfully, "Let's go fishing!"

Alex spent the rest of the day with her fishing rod in her hand pulling fish after fish out of the ocean. She tossed the fish to the Ocelots, one by one. Each would swallow it in one bite and then with a final *Meow* turned toward the direction of the jungle and head home.

Finally all of the Ocelots were fed and it was just Alex and Cookie left. They sat on the grassy edge of the bank of the river. What an amazing adventure this had been, thought Alex.

She put her hand on Cookie's soft head and said, "Should we go home and see the kittens or are you up for one last adventure?"

She knew that the kittens were now safe because the villager would still be there to take care of them. Cookie said, "Meow" in agreement.

"C'mon," said Alex.

They were still close to the extreme mountain biome. They walked back easily and Alex looked up again at the tall peak they had seen the previous day.

I bet Steve is still in there, thought Alex.

She and Cookie began to climb up and up. Soon they had

clouds surrounding them. At the very top, sure enough, there was the start of the black hole of a tunnel going straight into the mountain.

Alex looked down into the darkness uncertainly. Then she took a deep breath and jumped in. Down and down she went. Occasionally there was a torch on the wall that lit the way. Finally she landed on a stone floor with a thump.

There were three tunnels in front of her. Steve must have run into some trouble finding his emeralds. Which one should she go down?

She went to the opening of the first tunnel and looked into it. It was lit with torches and the floor was lined with track. At the top of the track was a minecart. It was full of coal.

Hmm, he must have had no luck with this tunnel, thought Alex. She looked at the next opening. It was dark but looked more promising.

Alex took a torch from the wall and went in a little ways. She soon found herself at the edge of a giant lava pit.

One side of the wall was lined with stone steps that were elevated above the burning mass of swirling fire.

Alex jumped to the first step. *Steve better be down here,* she thought to herself. Keeping a careful eye out for the lava she made her way to each step with Cookie following closely behind.

At last she was on solid bedrock. On either side of the tunnel were small rooms where Steve had attempted to mine. They looked abandoned.

At last, up ahead, she saw the glow of more torches and something green?

Then she heard the unmistakable sound of the tapping of a pickaxe. Alex went from the narrow tunnel and entered an enormous room. It glittered with emeralds. She stood looking up, dazzled by their brilliance.

Chapter 12

"Alex? What are you doing here?" she heard Steve's voice.

Alex looked around and then up. Steve was perched in an alcove at the top of the room, looking down at her.

"Oh, hey Steve," she said as casually as she could. "Cookie and I thought it would be fun to see what you were up to."

"Well, as you can see," said Steve proudly, "I found the

mother-lode. I've been down here for weeks."

"Yes, I can see," said Alex.

"How are things on the farm?" said Steve. "Anything exciting happening?" he added a little sarcastically.

"Oh, actually an angry Griefer sent a Creeper army to destroy the Overworld," replied Alex.

"What?" said Steve startled.

Alex told him the whole story of what had happened. How she and Cookie had snuck past the Creepers into the End Portal, the scary Griefer with his awful Creeper skin, the Endermen, and then how Cookie and the Ocelots

70

had pushed the Creeper army back into the mountain.

Steve said he was shook in his underground cave by the TNT explosion but didn't know what it was. He stared at Alex in awe.

"All that was going on while I've been down here!?" he exclaimed. "I missed it all!" He shook his head sadly.

Alex and Steve made their way back to the vertical tunnel chamber. Steve gave Alex a huge amount of Emerald and promised to visit her once he was finished in his mine.

It turned out the third tunnel was actually a horizontal way out of the mountain. Steve explained that it actually was kind of a pain going straight through the top of a mountain after all.

Alex and Steve high-fived their goodbyes and then Alex and Cookie walked out of the mountain.

When they emerged into the bright sunlight of the mountain biome, Alex turned to Cookie and said, "Let's go home!"

Cookie said, "Meow" and began to run in the direction of

the forest and their snug little
house beyond.

Chapter 13

When Alex and Cookie arrived at the house, Mr. Long Nose was outside with the kittens. He was sitting in the grass looking as stiff as a board.

The kittens were jumping from his head to his folded arms to his legs. They had clearly found a new obstacle course!

Cookie ran up to them with a loud, *Meow*. The kittens stopped in their tracks and greeted her with dozens of Meows and kisses.

Alex knelt to greet Sugar, Chip and Bob. Predictably, Sugar nuzzled her hand, Chip wanted to be scratched on the chin and Bob jumped up on her leg and began to climb up her hair.

"Bob!" she scolded. It was good to be home.

Mr. Long Nose said that he was becoming concerned that she and Cookie had not been home earlier. He had sustained some scratches and had had a nasty fall when he was forced to chase Bob, who had run into the forest.

Alex told him all about what had happened and how she and Cookie had narrowly averted a disaster. Mr. Long Nose listened, wide-eyed in disbelief. Then, Alex gave him a large sack of emeralds in payment for his kitten-sitting.

Mr. Long Nose was more than pleased. He had never had such an amount of treasure before and there was a skip in his step as he turned to walk back toward his village.

Alex and Cookie rounded up the kittens and brought them into the house.

Alex fed everyone their fish dinner and then began to unpack her inventory.

She put her diamond sword in its special chest, and then the iron pickaxe and fishing rod in theirs. Last she unpacked the remaining emeralds that Steve had given her and lay them before her. They cast a beautiful, luminous green light. It made her think of all the green Creepers they had encountered on their adventure.

Alex wondered if that sad Griefer would ever be back. It could return in another form. If it did she would have to be ready.

In the meantime, she would see what she could trade for all these emeralds.

And, she thought as she looked at Cookie and her playful kittens, there is so much fishing to do!

The End

If you haven't already done so, be
sure to read the first Alex and
Cookie book: *Alex and Cookie
Save Steve* and then check out
Herobrine's Curse.

About Blockerella

I'm a die-hard Minecraft fan and a gal! I love the Alex skin and want to help other fans discover how great she is. If you like this story and haven't already seen it, look for the first book in the series, *Alex and Cookie Save Steve*.

And, *please leave a review* of this book.

Thanks!

Printed in Great Britain
by Amazon